THE S... HORACE

Retold and illustrated by

ALICE M. COATS

FABER & FABER
24 Russell Square, London

First published in 1937
by Faber and Faber Limited
24 Russell Square London WC1
First published in this edition 1970
Printed in Great Britain by
Latimer Trend & Co Ltd, Whitstable
All rights reserved

SBN (paper edition) 571 09414 7
SBN (cloth edition) 571 05773 X

ONCE UPON A TIME

THERE WAS A FAMILY

who all lived together

in a little house in a wood.

There was:—

GREAT-GRANDPA,
GREAT-GRANDMA,

GRANDPA,
GRANDMA,

PA,
MA,

PAUL

and

little

LULU.

And with them lived HORACE.

HORACE

was a BEAR!

One day

Pa went out hunting.

And on the way back, he was met by—

GREAT-GRANDMA, GRANDPA, GRA

A, MA, PAUL and little LULU

And they all said,

"What do you think has happened?"

And Pa said,

"What

            HAS

                       happened?"

And they said;—·

"Horace has eaten

GREAT-GRANDPA!"

And Pa was just WILD,

and he said,

"I will KILL Horace!"

But they all took on so,

he hadn't the heart to do it.

Farewell!

And the next day

Pa went out hunting.

And on the way back, he was met by—

GRANDPA, GRANDMA,

MA, PAUL and little LULU.

And they all said,

"What do you think has happened?"

And Pa said,

"What

has

happened?"

And they said:—

"Horace has eaten

GREAT-GRANDMA!"

And Pa was just WILD,

and he said,

"I will KILL Horace!"

But they all took on so,

he hadn't the heart to do it.

And the next day

Pa went out hunting.

And on the way back, he was met by—

GRANDMA,

MA, PAUL and little LULU

And they all said,

"What do you think has happened?"

And Pa said,

"What

HAS

happened?"

And they said;—

"Horace has eaten

GRANDPA!"

And Pa was just WILD,

and he said,

"I will KILL Horace!"

But they all took on so,

he hadn't the heart to do it.

And the next day

Pa went out hunting.

And on the way back

he was met by

MA,

    PAUL

        and

           little

              LULU.

And they all said,

"What do you think has happened?"

And Pa said,

"WHAT

        has

                happened?"

And they said:—

"Horace has eaten

GRANDMA!"

And Pa was just WILD,

and he said,

"I will KILL Horace!"

But they all took on so,

he hadn't the heart to do it.

And the next day

Pa went out hunting.

And on the way back

he was met by

PAUL

and

little

LULU.

And they both said,

"What do you think has happened?"

And Pa said,

"What

HAS

happened?"

And they said:—

"Horace has eaten

MA!"

And Pa was just WILD,

and he said,

"I will KILL Horace!"

But they both took on so,

he hadn't the heart to do it.

And the next day

Pa went out hunting.

And on the way back

he was met by

little

LULU

And little Lulu said,

"What do you think has happened?"

And Pa said

"WHAT

HAS

HAPPENED?"

And little Lulu said:—

"Horace has eaten

PAUL!"

And Pa was just WILD,

and he said,

"I WILL KILL HORACE!"

But little Lulu took on so,

he hadn't the heart to do it.

And the next day

Pa went out hunting.

And on the way back

he was met by

HORACE!

And Horace said,

"What do you think has happened?"

And Pa said,

?

"WHAT

HAS

HAPPENED?"

And Horace said:—

"I've eaten

LITTLE LULU!"

And Pa was just WILD,

and he said,

"I will kill you, Horace"!

But HORACE took on so—

he hadn't the heart to do it.

And the next day

HORACE

went out hunting!

IN LOVING MEMORY
OF
GREAT-GRANDPA
GREAT-GRANDMA
GRANDPA, GRANDMA
MA, PAUL
LITTLE LULU
&
PA,

THIS STONE WAS ERECTED
BY THEIR SORROWING
HORACE